# SEX
# & THE
# SINGLE GIRL
# REVISITED

Just what is on
your mind, girlfriend?

by anand
with additional illustrations
by bernarda saldo
and friends

Library of Congress Cataloging-in-Publication Data
Stratton, Mary-Margaret (anand sahaja)
Sex & the Single Girl Revisited

Summary: "Just what is on your mind, girlfriend? a collection of writings written about clandestine situations that I have witnessed... imagined... or quite possibly experienced..." – Provided by the publisher.

ISBN-13: 978-0-9998749-5-0
ISBN-10: 0-9998749-5-0

1. Literature and Fiction >

Published by Futura House
2620 South Maryland Parkway #345
Las Vegas, NV 89109
Printed in the United States of America
www.futurahouse.com
Book Design and Images by MM Stratton (megorama.com)
using American Typewriter

# table of contents

# dedication

to the muses of charles bukowski
and e.e. cummings.
to jeanne farrens.

# fore-words

a collection of writings written about
clandestine situations that I have either
witnessed...
imagined...
or quite possibly experienced...

# **"Yes, I have a boyfriend."**

I said in answer to his question.

hypnotic pulsating
red blue green lights
gold chain glittering
woofers pounding,
"What is love?
baby don't hurt me..."
He asked me if I'd cheat...

Disco is not dead.

## swim

we got out of the Jacuzzi
and dove into the pool
to 'cool off.'

it may have worked for a while
but soon my backstroke
went awry and
we collided in the deep end.

# <u>Winning</u>

This guy I dated
was always trying to
pick a fight with me.
He said I was difficult
to argue with...

...that I never tried to win.

I wouldn't contradict him.
It drove him crazy.

He was wrong.
I won.

# **RRR**

Ravenous
Ravishing
Radishes

Never cared much for them myself
But some people like them

I don't know?
Ask Dr. Ruth.

Some people are willing
to stuff anything in their mouth
just to fill a void.

# Fire Engines

3 fire engines
and a dirty little old man
at the corner
where I biked.

I asked him
what went on?
he said something
about a fire in the elevator
then looked at my legs
and said something about
exercise and
looking good.

I left quickly
it was getting a
little too hot
in the old neighborhood.

## wet

breasts too tender
to touch.
cold hard sheets.
eyes closed to all
but the black upon black
back shadow-y
corners of the room.
lower back aches
for a pressure
from within.

come to me.
i am waiting.
hold me.
i am woman.
take me now.
i am wanting.
do to me.
i am willing.

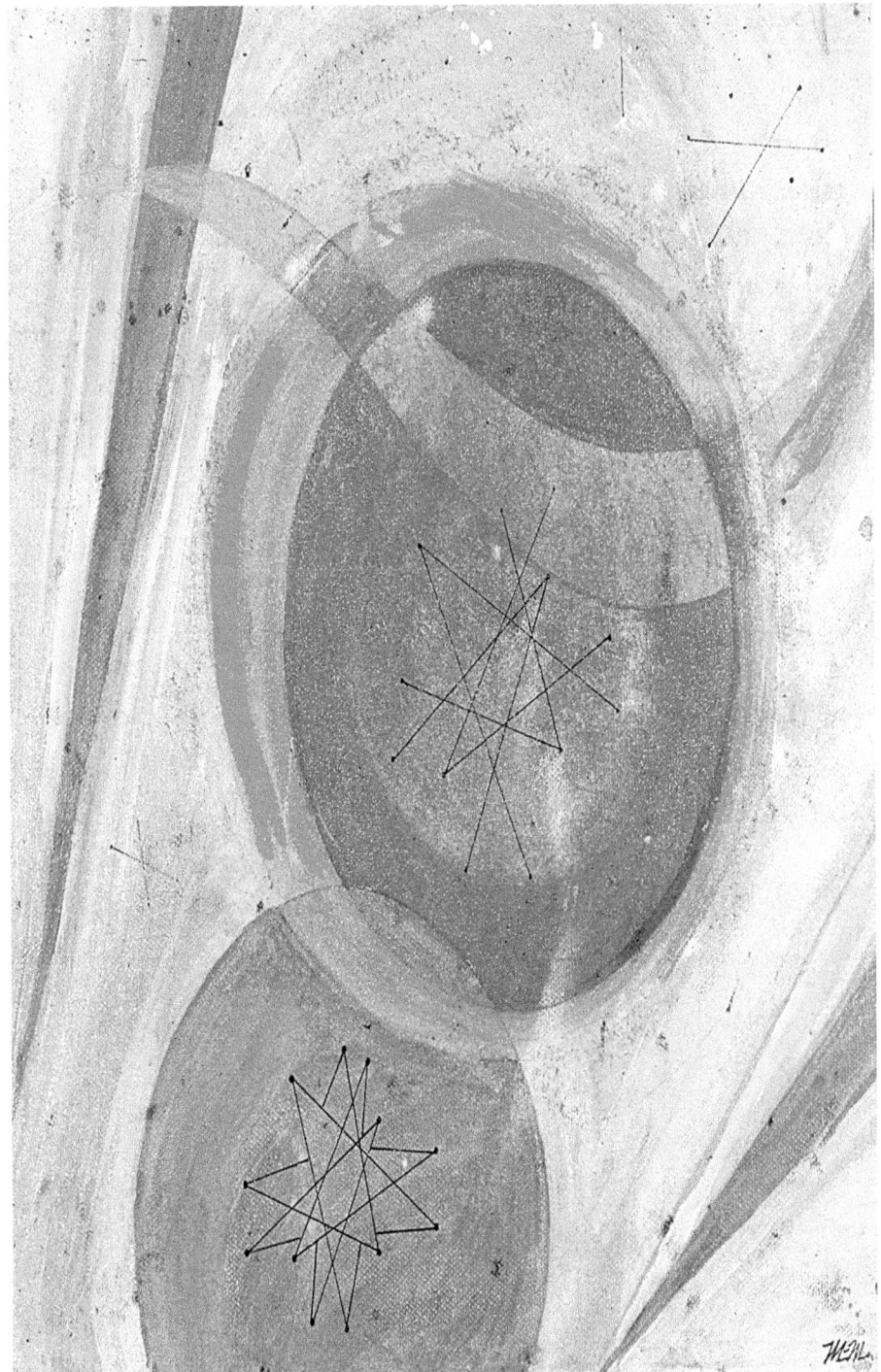

# **Off**

so he's off
with his guy friends
then getting off
with some girl friend

and to think
he was inches away...
all we needed was a little G-force
and we would have been off
and rinning.

it turns me off
to think he's off
only because i said, "no"
once too
off-ten

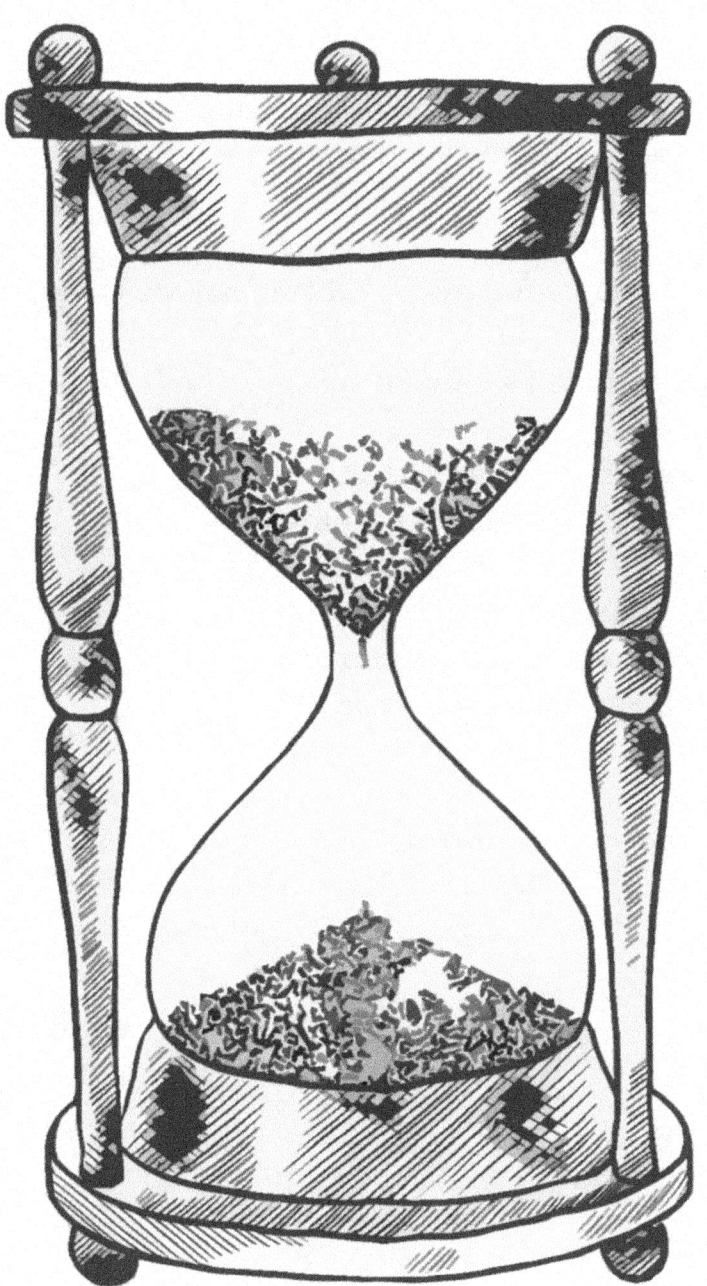

# I Scream

Tonight I wanted this night to be ours
Be on top of the world looking down
At the lights of the city
The power of the wind knocking us down
With an almost full moon lighting our way.

You just wanted a banana split.

Here I am in some stranger's
Dirty crappy apartment parking lot
Almost full moon setting in my eyes
The engine is running
You are ready to take me home
And you ask me what's wrong?

I yell,
"You had your ice cream."

# missing your vibes

we go way back
you and i.
alone late at night
after everyone had gone to sleep
you were the best lover I ever had.
touched me just the right
ways I wanted with
the perfect hand,
the perfect motion.

how sad I was when you left.
for years I searched to find another,
but no one is ever like the first.
Sadly,
when a good motor goes bad
there is no electronic Viagra.

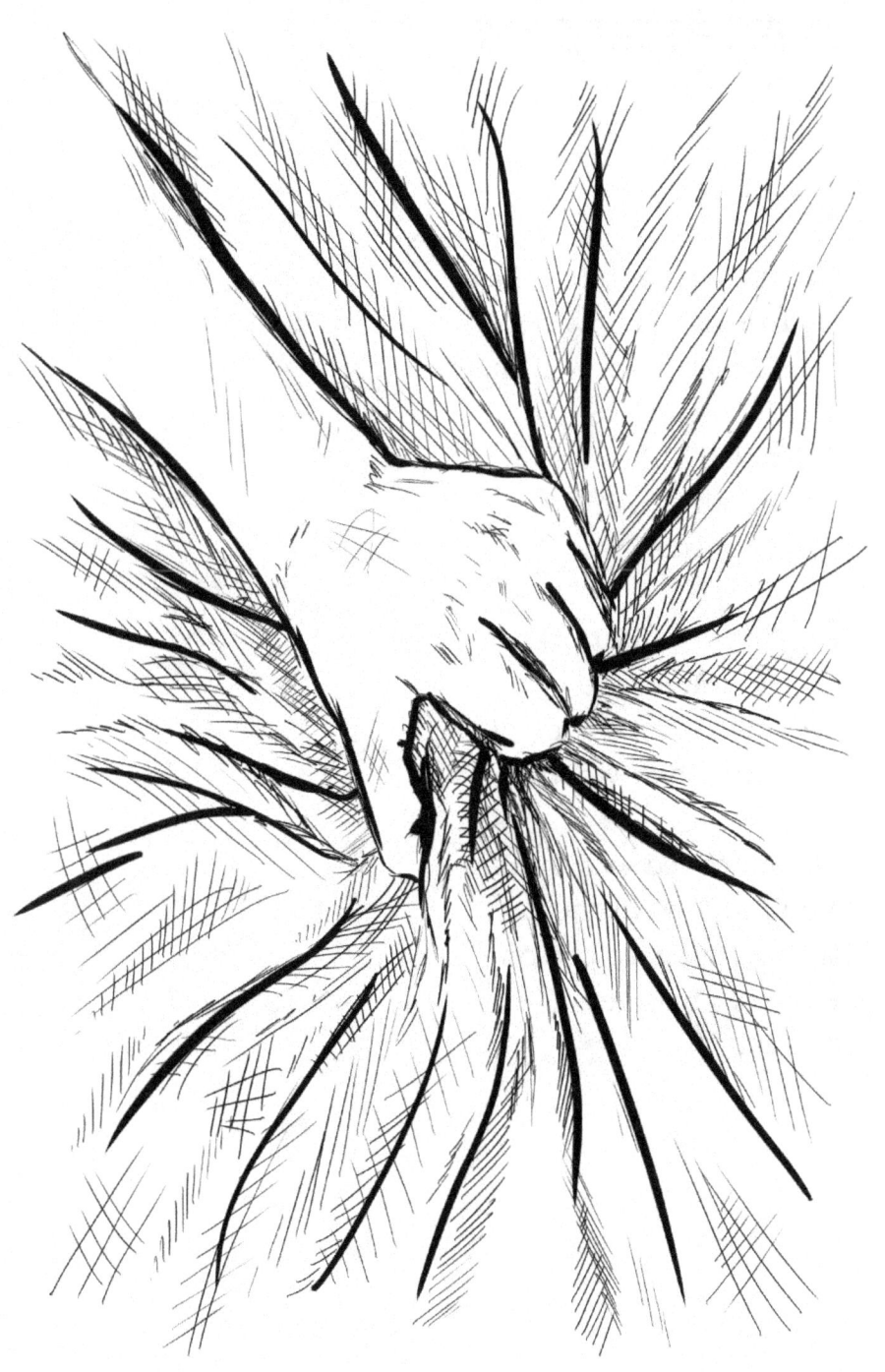

# Asti Spumonte

Asti Spumonte
sparkling wine

You shared your share and
we drank the bottle...
or at least what was inside

Then you shared even more
on the dirt path
by your car

As the headlights passed
on the other side
I came to sit beside you
and crouched wobbly

Light headed and bubbly
You laughed at me
When you were the one
who lost balance
and fell.

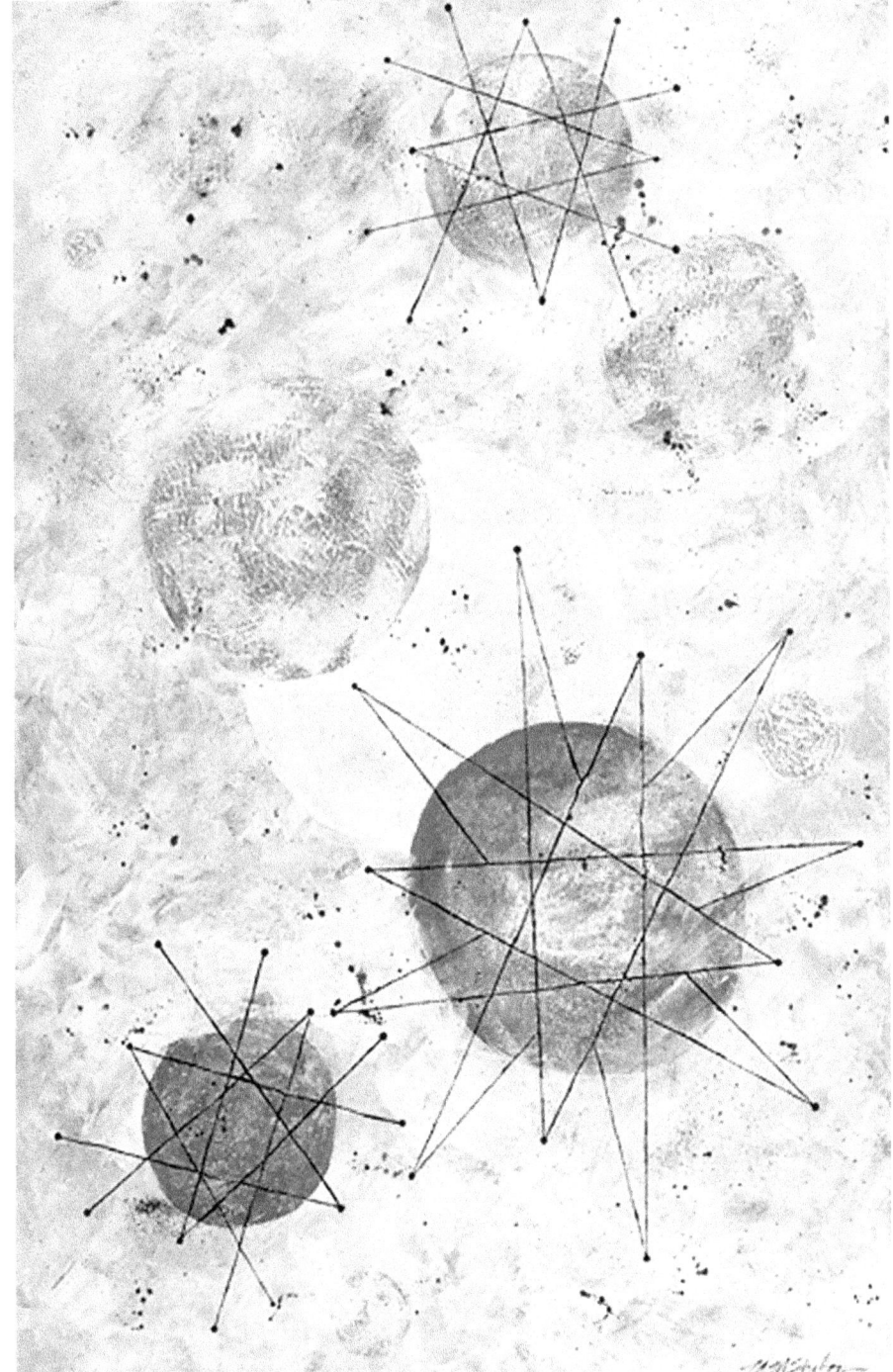

# I Want More

I want to wear exactly what
They wear in fashion magazines.
I want to go out every night
Spend money makin' silly scenes.

I want the five star service
Cause the people know my name.
I want to be the one on top,
'Cause I plan to win this game.

I want something for fingers
Big, bright and super real,
But there's one bigger thing
That I really want to feel.

I want a house and a nice yard,
And a pretty cool car, too,
But really most of all
I want more sex from you.

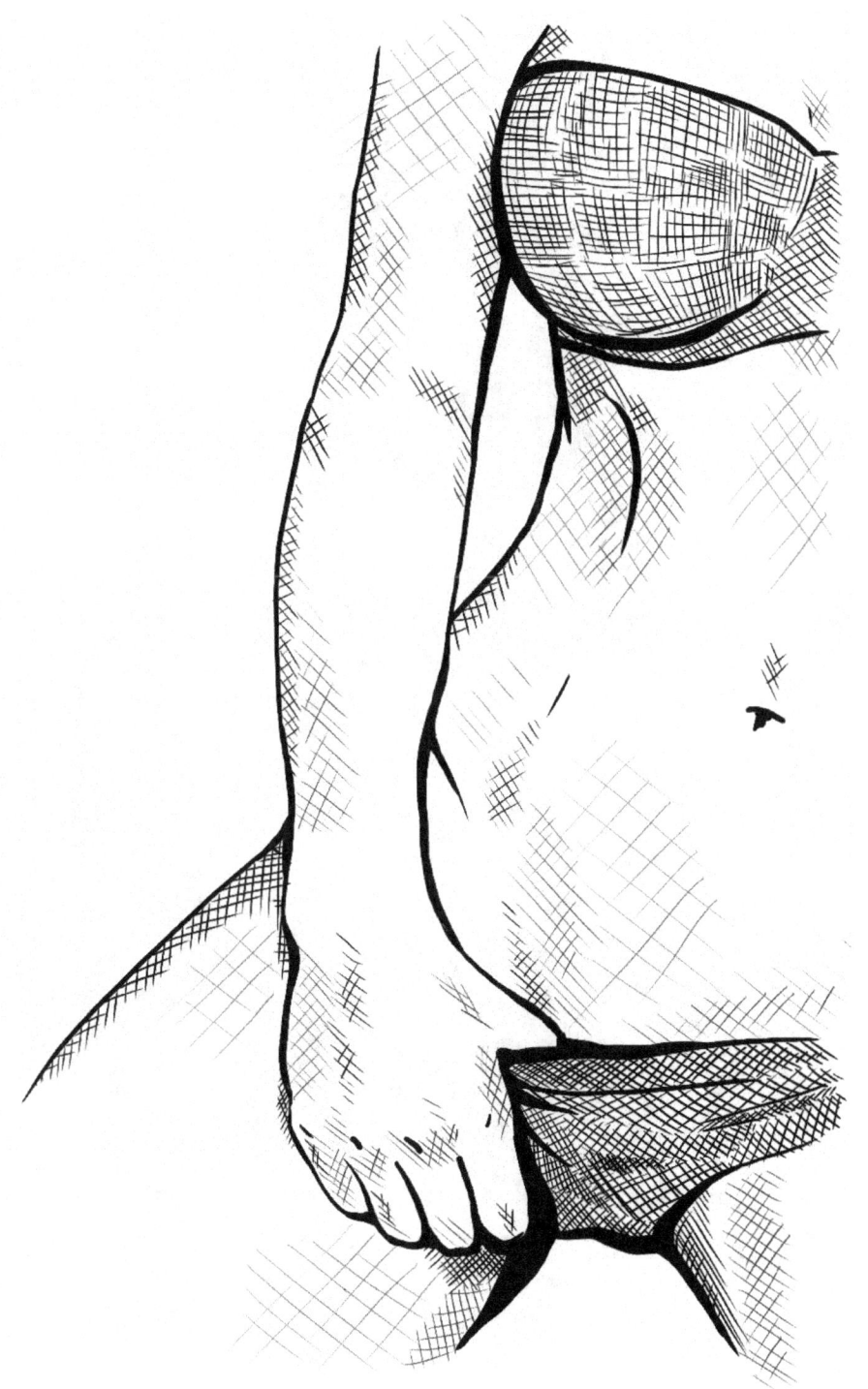

# Problems with Superiority

I need your strength
to wrap its arms around me

And I need you to suffocate me
with your familiar breath

And I need you to pressure me
to submit to your equality

Most of all
I need you near me, around me
between the folds of my flesh

I'm lazy
let me be beneath you.

# sacrifice

what must i sacrifice
to have another
intimate moment
of your intensity?

how much must i give up
to get to where
i can give in
to your insistence?

why must i endure
endless unknowing
when a moment of your embrace
will suffice?

# Next Time... a Timer

The night I asked him to dinner
I meant it as a thank you
and a farewell.
It was all set up
perfect and platonic,
But he took over the tongs
and the steaks burned.

69

1234567

# A new Game

The night we played chess
in front of the fire
His bishop captured my queen
and he won.

And then he taught me backgammon
With a few rolls of the dice
I sped things up,
made my moves
and I won.

he said
it was beginner's luck.

it wasn't that...
I just like learning
new games.

# Carpenteria Pier

I remember his lips on the step that night.
I was the do-it-all age of fifteen.
His wiry arms were holding me tight.
He was an old man at age eighteen

He'd ride out beyond the pay Zuma surf
While I sat by on the sand and drew...
Feeling Deacon Blues in the coco-filled air
Making out in a green VW.

We were too young to know it could be more.
He went away a lost summer friend.
Found a reason to break it apart
As I said goodbye to innocent heart
That believed in a happy end.

Why wonder - why wonder – why?
Where did it all go?
The sound of the sea that I'd hear
Why wonder - why wonder – why?
We let it all go
Under the Carpenteria Pier.

# green tea time

We slow dance in the heat
of a summer evening.

the candle steadies its flickering
and stretches sensuously.

my eyes reflect the flame when you look at me.
The smell of ginger lingers in the heat.

And the tea cups lie turned
where we told our fortunes.

# Harlot Starlet

red toenails
she laughs and
teases the gathered

purple hat dipped
below one eye
she gives them the image
they asked for.
and keeps an eye on it
in the mirror

when they want more
she must deny them
and leave them begging.

a woman in red toenails
doesn't really mean it
never enough of her to go around.

So they move on...
their attention gone
she pouts, then smiles

who can be serious
in red toenails?

# good karma

watching you eloquently
handle chopsticks
I pondered.


when you left
you turned to smile at me.
I must have some
good karma.

good Karma
San Jose
1-25-09

# virgin haiku

champagne satin
her shiny dreams
slide off the sheets

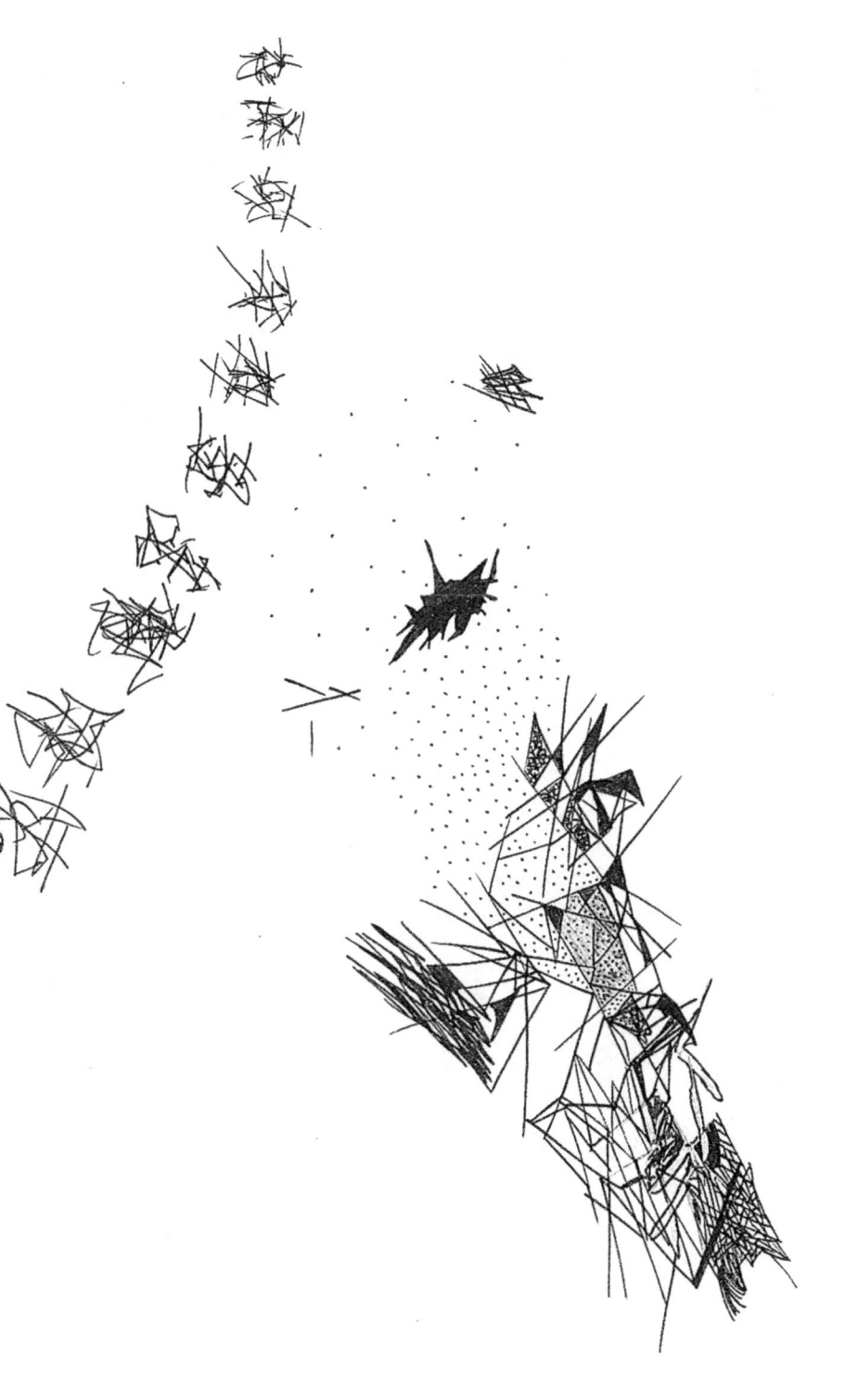

# futile graffiti

Crowded around a club mirror

We stand
In high heels
Works of our own art
To be selected
By an indiscriminate and
Aesthetically-challenged audience

Popular Girls

## control

Ambitious for her alcoholic.
sight of self, unseen.

she plans the present
for him,

wiles ways to be
by him,

gives gladly
to him,

thinking all along

he's the one
who has
lost control.

# frozen fingers

cold hands - warm heart
they say.

it's true.

My fingers are always frozen.
toes too.
but i'm far from frigid.

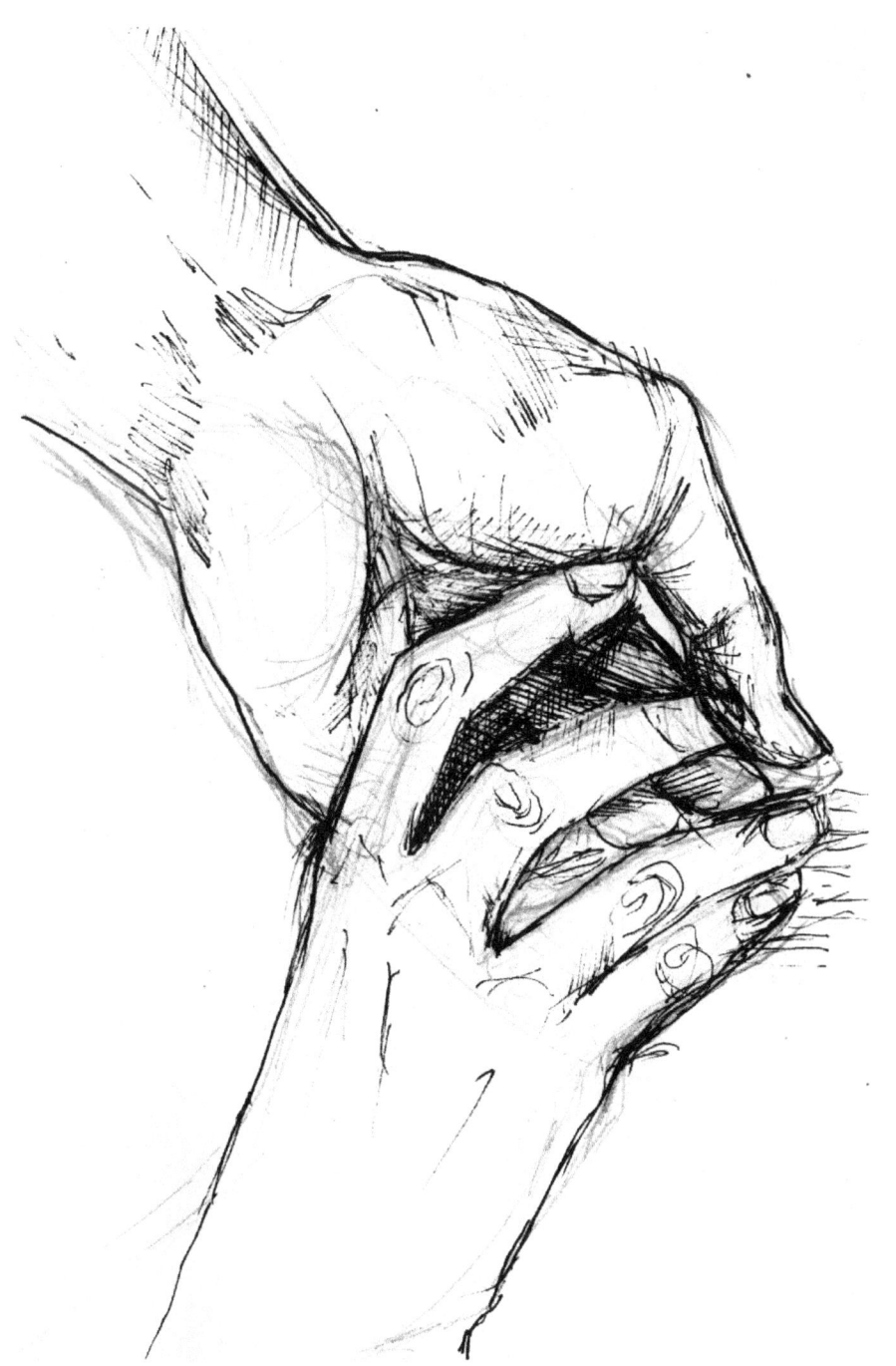

# Men in Black Cars

men in black cars
unknowingly aspire to
fascist superiority

sometimes knowingly...
charcoal glass
screens out glares

a woman who loves too much
always wants
the man in black,
the Darth Maul mask
cool exterior an enticement
for masochistic actions.

I want one.
My boot in the face man
encased in a black box
holds the bait:

the desire for submission.

# to fillip

we fumbled
I froze
you laffed at
my feelings
but finally
we fell
and you felt
like the first

my fear is fading
fast.
Madonna
wasn't so far
off track
after all.

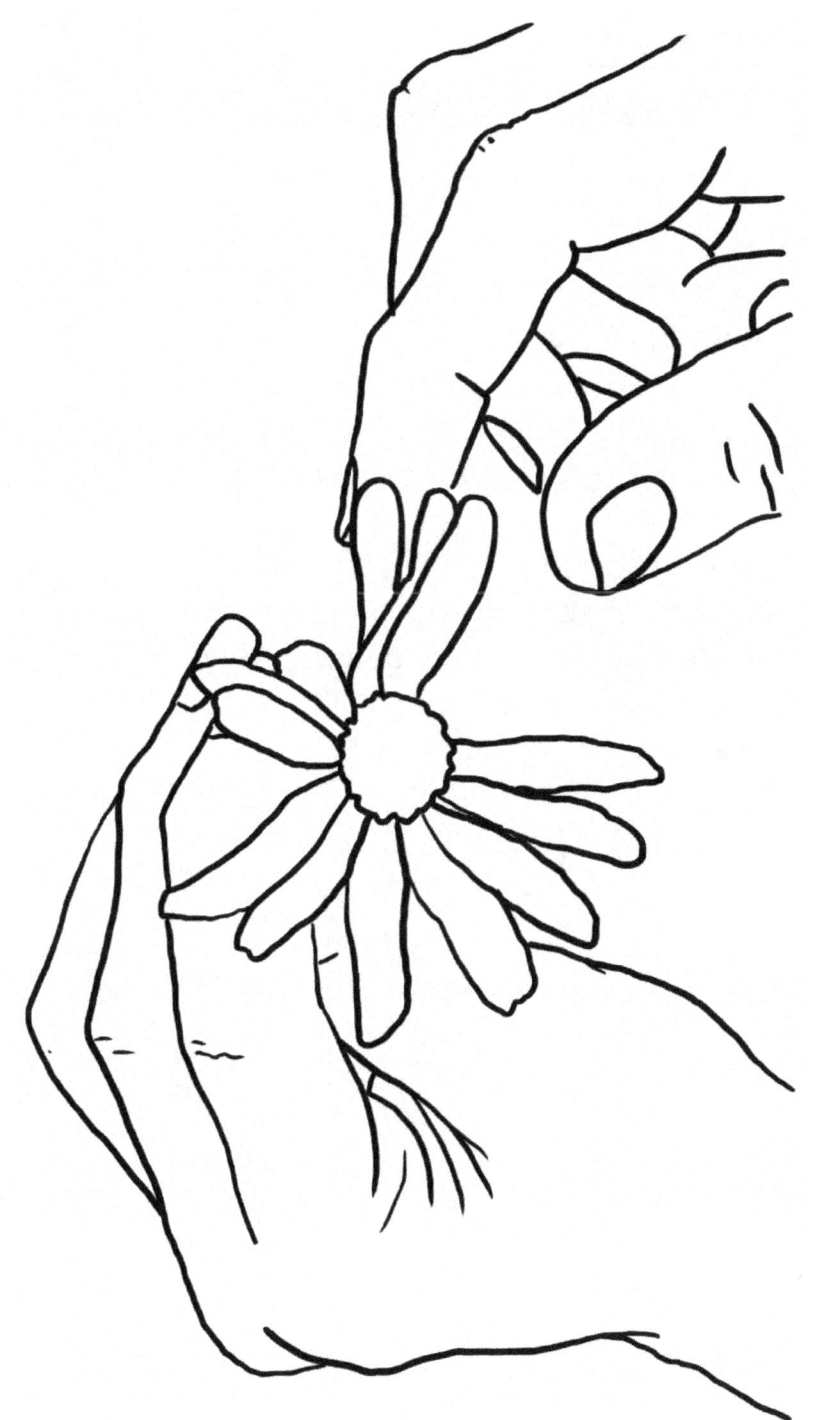

# woman in a creampuff cadillac

*(dedicated to charles bukowski)*

Being driven around by a woman
in a creampuff cadillac
is like a goblet of champagne
tiny bubbles bursting under the nose
and a nasty hangover the day after.

being driven around by a woman
in a creampuff cadillac
is like eating spicy Italian sausage
zesty to the tastebuds and
a pain in the ass in the end.

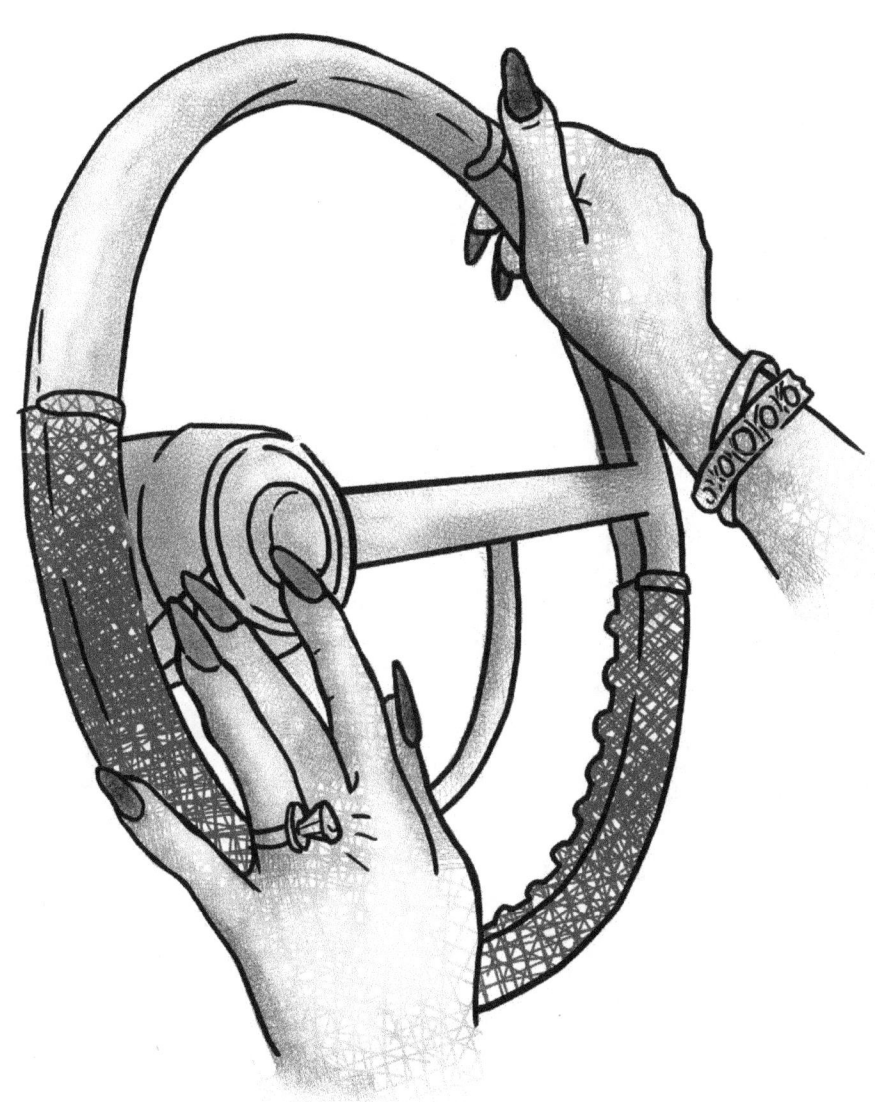

# ring

press
swipe-swipe
ringer's
on

press
swipe-swipe
any
thing?

press
swipe-swipe
almost
dawn

press
swipe-swipe
please please
ring.

Mt. Vernon Phone!

## tennis?

I warned him
I hadn't played in a while.
"It's been a couple of years at least,"
I said.

So we got to it
and actually
I hadn't lost my touch.
He said I had pretty good form
and helped me improve my strokes.

And in the end
I had the advantage.

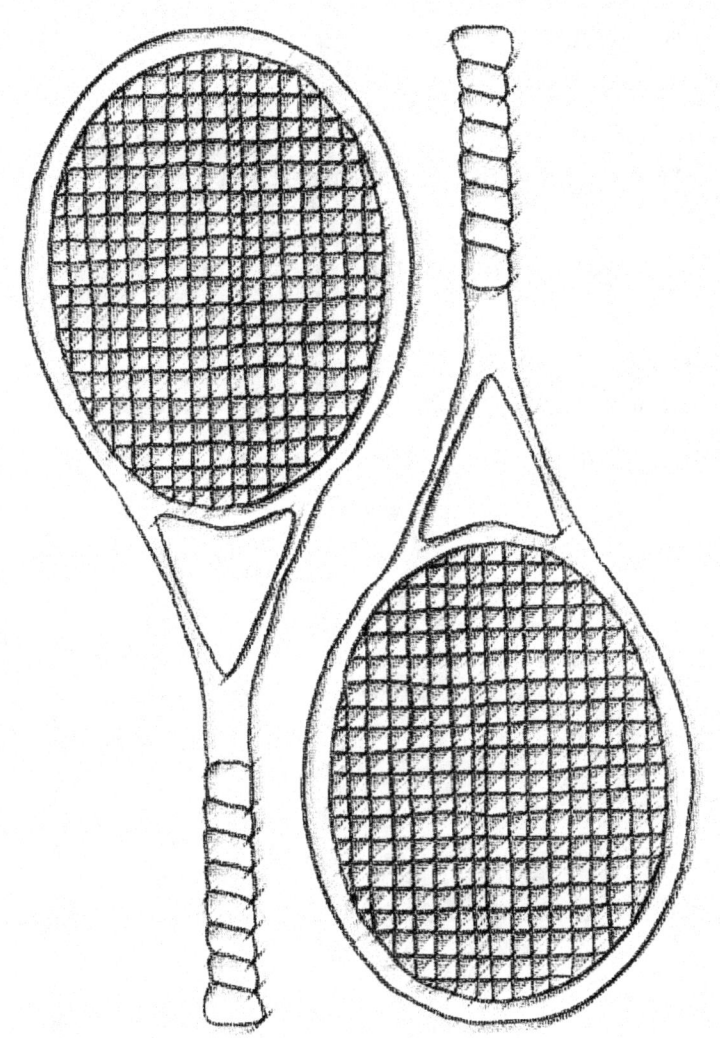

# green pants

green pants
with one bright brass button
And he accused me of staring?
Talk about a twist
We are talking loud green here.

And I wasn't supposed to look?

It was such a relief
when they finally came off.

# Below Blue Jay Way

Somewhere below Blue Jay Way
The city sparkles beyond.
The sagebrush quivers,
The far lights shimmer,
The man in the moon looks on.

I came here many times before
To drink and ignore the view
Now such magic is here,
In the sandalwood air,
And there's a need to subdue.

I wondered where love had gone
As the lights of Le Dome have waned,
But everything's clear
We are meant to be here
Together until the dawn.

Youth tapped me on the shoulder tonight
Inviting me to ride and I just might
Run off again with you,
Like we did when love was new.

# mini

I met him
Driving up the hill
At the crest of a curve
He was in a jag-U-ar.

Top down and shivering
I jumped out in my short skirt
Gave him my number
And in a spilt second
Fate made a fast turn
Downhill.

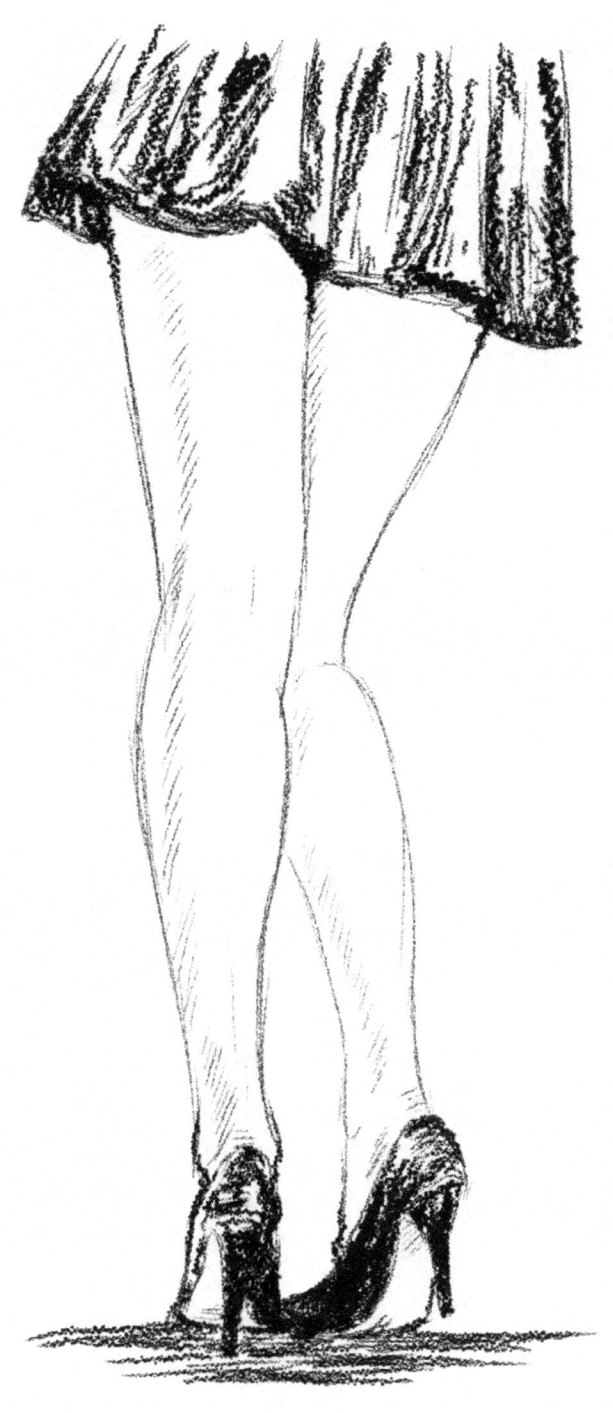

# machine gun man

I want a man
with a machine gun grinning
from ear to ear
as he blows
all my troubles
away.

# <u>drunk</u>

drunk
he nearly falls off his chair.
slurs "kiss me"
and then
misses me

sober
i fall into
tapioca dreams
soft sweet
sticky remembrances

i thought i had finally
given him up
and yet here i find myself
craving again.

# I Don't Love You

and I don't think I ever will.
You are not my ideal
and I won't give up anything for you.
But when I'm with you it's another story,
because...
You don't love me and probably never will.
I am not your ideal
and you won't give yourself to me.

so I want you.

# I used to

I used to
write a lot
on pads of paper
like this.
I used to
do lots
of things,
creatively speaking.
then things
stopped inspiring me
as life continued
becoming more infrequently impressive
'til I began to say,
"I used to"
a lot.
At that point
I didn't do
any-thing
and was not
aroused to try.

But then I saw this paper
looking so virgin
it reminded me
of how
I used to
be

# on and ON

pimento in an empty glass
on the pool table
bourbon
on his breath
and billiards
on our minds

then he made a remark
on how well I
maneuvered the balls
and handled...
the pool cue

we cleared the table.

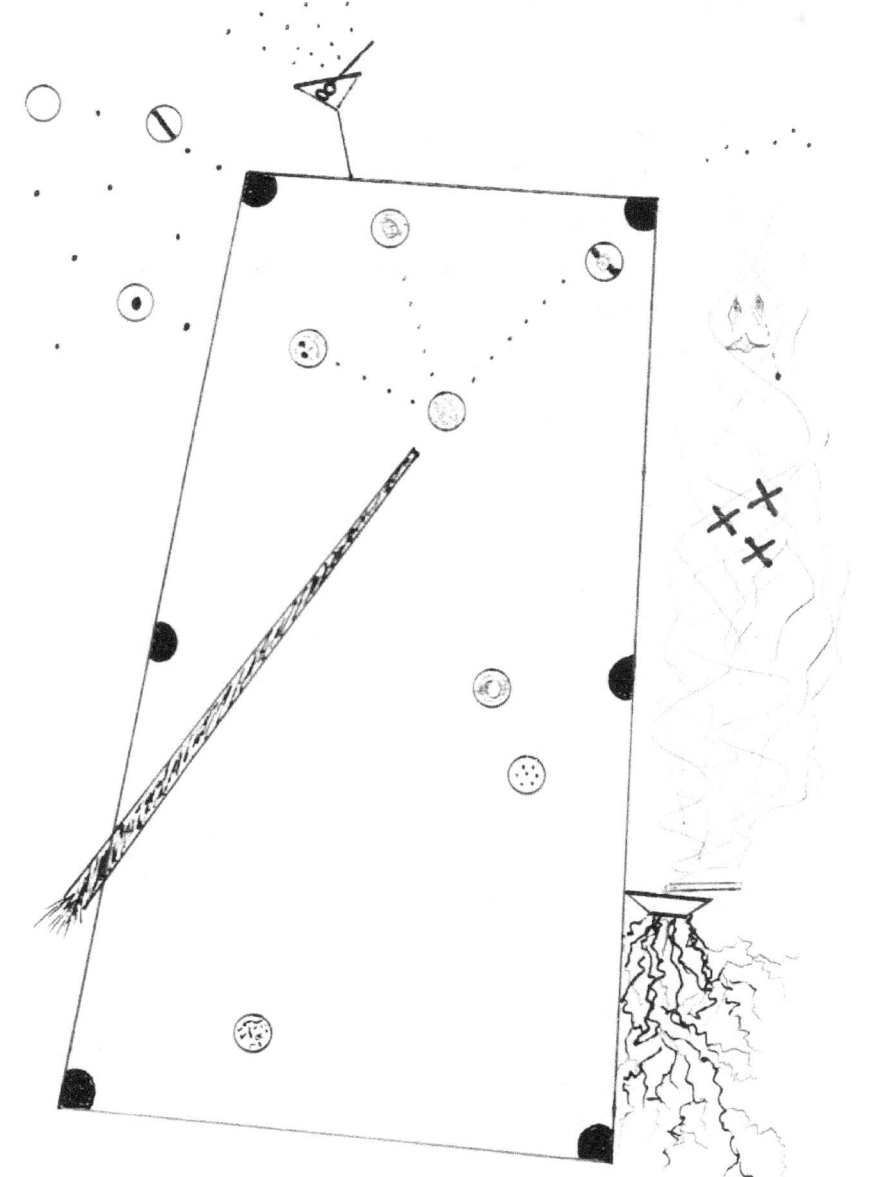

# graveyard

we drove past the graveyard
and you imagined yourself
surrounded with white light,
but you forgot to remind me to do the same
so there I was again,
vulnerable and with you.

## getaway

the single life
is long long gone
married doldrums
setting in.

when the home turf
doesn't cut it
hotel, motel,
Upham Inn.

Two
Chair          at the Upham
                 6-22-16

# next door to nothing

glass to the wall
they loudly parade
their inadequacy.

(the neighbors are having sex again)

gulping for a breath of life...
for anything real...
within the realm of my own senses.

I have looked for anything,
anywhere to arouse
my needs for
self-stimulus

i say "blah" to it all.
I say 'blah'
to the overdone theatrics next door.
i am simply a poet without the ability
to satisfy my own niche
of reality.

My room remains silent.

# By the Light of the Moon

They met in the night
One life lost and one gained
Passed an etude of time
They hoped would never end

He held her face in his hands
And her heart knew how to feel
But they both knew it was far too soon
As they danced by the light of the moon
The moon
They danced by the light of the moon

Ten hours went by
As the sun began to show.
In a fleeting moment a stranger
Becomes the closest that you know

# ego girl

do you think i don't know
about your many loving friends
with beautiful faces and meager minds
you try to mold?

do you think i don't know
how they disappoint you with roses
and accolades
when all you really wanted was
to run through an open field of flowers?

do you think i don't know
how you used up all the fakery inside you
and didn't want to climb back into
your empty shell?

do you think i don't know
about the mascara stains on your pillow
from the self-pity of who you
thought you were?

do you think i don't know
that you know your life up until now
has been a pretense, and only now
are you just beginning to know?
I know - because i am you.

# power tools

i never wanted to go through
the heart havoc again,
but the feeling is back
and there you are
ready to turn on,
ready to plug in,
grind me,
nail me,
screw me
again.

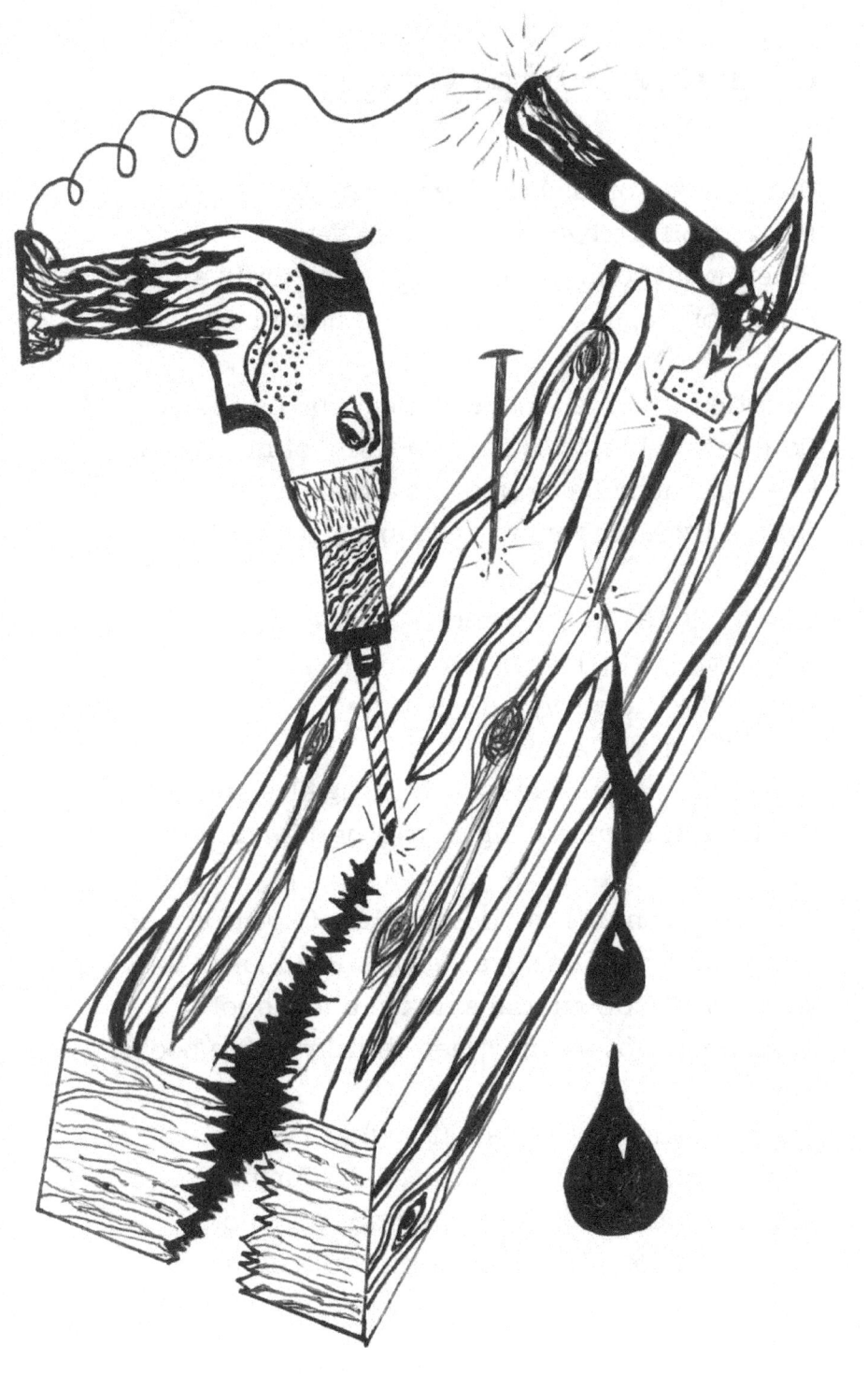

# Chunky White Chick

Out at a bar on a slow Tuesday night
Me and Bill Dubya trying not to get tight
When what to my wondering eyes should appear
A big boned gal - I'm gonna buy her a beer.

I nestled up on a stool and stuck by her side.
Couldn't help notice the rounding of her thigh.
She had the balls to wear not much at all.
Lean a little closer hun - I wanna see it all.

Don't like the skinny ones –
Afraid they slip away.
Don't like the curvy ones –
Can't trust 'em anyway.
The chunkier the better - Nothing else will do,
'Cause I like something - I can handle onto.

I asked her name 'n does she like Garth Brooks?
She looked me once over, gave the all right look.
We got right down and smoked a few doobs,
And then I got to know her chunky white boobs.

The chunkier the better. It's what I like.
She'll look just right on the back of my bike.
She'd the kinda girl who pours it on thick
Just my style, she's a chunky white chick

---

# urge

i feel the urge
the urge to merge.

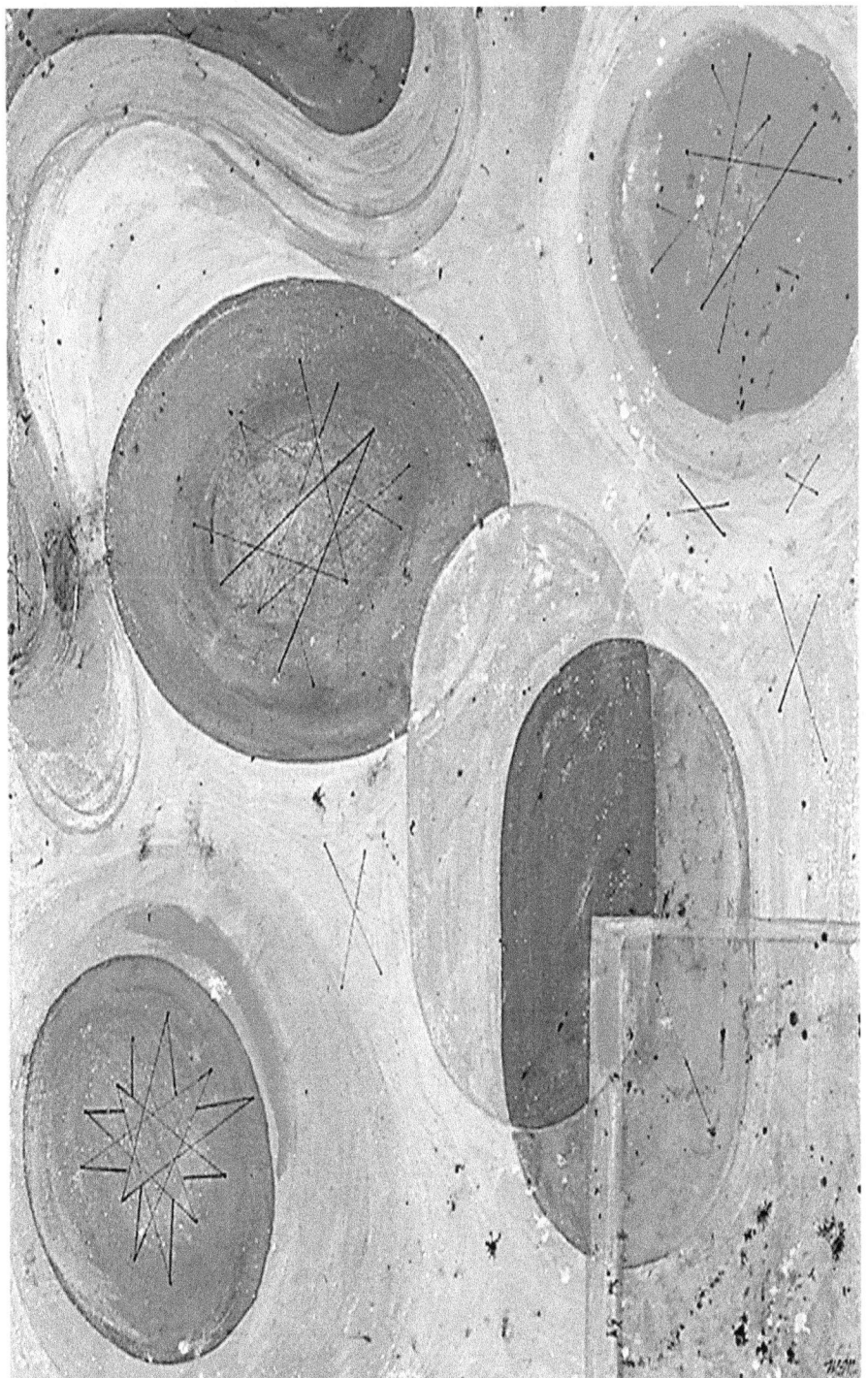

# about the author~illustrator

anand has been published by Westwind - UCLA's Journal of the Arts, Manuscript Magazine, Seventeen Magazine, and other journals of creative writing. She enjoys writing short and punchy, irreverent and insightful  poetry and prose. By day she is a professional creative communications consultant. By night, a musician and artist. She longs to spend a year in Paris painting, and a year in Manhattan painting the town.

anandsahaja.com

## other works by anand:

Non Fiction

Dominant Health
Eat Like Eve
The Good Wiccan Guides
How Modern Was
   My Valley
Kiss Addiction Goodbye
Kiss Addiction Away
Marry & Grow Happy
Mondo Vegas
Pop Tags – Volumes 1&2
Stop Picking on Me
SPOM Workbook
The SoLa SoFiA Method

Fiction/Prose

Endings?
An Heirloom Adventure
My Life As An Angel
One Toy, Two Toys, Too
   Many Shoo Toys
Please Don't Eat My
   Friends
Sex & Single Girl
   Revisited
Wheel of the Year
Why Am I?

# about the illustrator

Bernarda Saldo hails from Croatia. She likes coffee, dogs, South Park, sunsets and bread, in no particular order! She is a trained illustrator and especially loves to work in the black and white mode in both an abstract and literal style. She feels, "There is a special bond between poetry and illustration."

Instagram: crtamito

~ pages   9, 13, 17, 21, 25, 31, 35, 39, 53, 59, 61, 63, 65, 69, 71, 89

# additional illustrators

Alen Burazerovic is an illustrator with an MFA in printmaking, and a animator from Bosnia and Herzegovina. Instagram/alenburazerovic ~ pages 47, 51, 77, 83

Angela Li James is a student of architecture in the Central University of Venezuela ~ page 49

Aruti Desh is an Indian artist and the author of Unwind: To the Joy of Coloring ~ page 29

Bianca Stancu is a watercolor painter and bird enthusiast from Romania. behance.net/inking_dove ~ page 19, 37, 55

Cary Brian Stratton ~ CBS aka Chef Mason Green is an accomplished performer and artist. CaryStratton.com ~ page 43, 67, 75, 87

Oksana Didkova is an ink and watercolor artist from the Ukraine ~ page 81

Poulomi Mondal has a degree in graphic design from St. Xavier's College in India facebook.com/skylantern23 ~ page 5, 11

Thank you for listening.